All The Guys

One Woman / Multiple Men
A Collection of Five Short Stories

By

Emma Jade

All The Guys:
One Woman / Multiple Men
A Collection of Five Short Stories

A Night Turned Threesome

When I turned 30, I was fortunate enough to have a husband who enjoyed sex as much as I did (well maybe not quite as much as I did cause I'm a slut ;). We frequently had shared birthday parties at our place and this year was no different. This one particular Saturday night, everyone seemed to be having a good time. There were about twenty people, including my husband, David, and me.

As the night wore on, I had a few drinks. I wasn't what you would call "drunk", but I was feeling no pain. During the evening, Abe, an old school friend showed up and I was speechless, I hadn't seen him in... forever... why did he show up? Furthermore, he was especially attentive towards me. He made many efforts to "accidentally" brush up against me. And he placed his hand on my back casually sliding it down over my ass. Or grabbing me for a quick kiss on the lips, pressing his chest against my tits.

I don't mind admitting that he was turning me on, and I could feel that my panties were moist. I was puzzled with his actions, but didn't really think to question them.

Around 2:00 a.m. everyone had left, leaving me, David, and Abe. The three of us were sitting on the sofa, talking with me in the middle. David pulled me closer and started kissing me. I could feel his hands sliding up and down my back. Then I felt a hand on my breast. I knew instantly that it wasn't David, so I turned and saw Abe smiling at me.

"Do you mind?" Abe asked.

I looked around at David, and he was smiling too.

"Not at all," I smiled back.

Abe's touch was so different from David's that my nipples were instantly erect. He had stopped rubbing, but left his hand cupping my tit. I shifted slightly causing his hand to move against my hard nipple. I couldn't help but moan softly as David leaned in to kiss me again.

All kinds of thoughts were flooding my mind. Was this really happening?

Abe moved up behind me and the two of them pulled me into a group hug of sorts, the only difference being, their hands were all over me. Abe cupped each of my tits into his huge hands. I had never seen such large hands on anyone! And I wondered if what I had heard was true? Big hands...big? David slid his hand up my skirt and was rubbing my pussy through my panties.

"Oh fuck," he said, "she's wet already!"

I let them lead me to the bedroom. My heart was racing as the two of them took turns removing articles of my clothing. I remember it being very sensuous because with each item they removed, they kissed and licked whatever skin was exposed.

Abe knelt before me and slid my panties down over my ass. As the cool air hit my pussy I could tell I was very wet. My nipples stood out begging for attention! I turned to each of them, removing their shirts and jeans.

David stood there in his boxer briefs and Abe was naked under his jeans. God I love that! At this point I was too turned on to even consider stopping what we were doing! Even if they wanted to!

I kneeled down between them. I watched David's hard cock spring forward as I pulled his boxer briefs down over his ass. It bounced as he stepped out of them.

Then I turned to Abe and wrapped my hand around the shaft of his hard thick cock. Mmmmmm, I was in heaven! I had a cock in each hand, demanding attention from me! I could feel my pussy getting wetter. I didn't know where to start, so I continued stroking both cocks in my hands.

Moving closer to David, I slid my tongue over the head of his cock. "Mmmmmm," he moaned the minute I made contact. I took his head into my mouth while I kept up my stroking of each shaft.

It was so hard to concentrate, but I managed. Then I moved over to Abe's cock. The head filled my mouth. He was much thicker than David, where David was longer. The best of both worlds!

At one point, I tried to take the heads of both cocks into my mouth. I don't know if they liked the idea of their cocks touching, but I had always wanted to do that and I was in control. That felt great! I moved my tongue around both heads and they soon forgot their trepidation. I was sucking and licking them at the same time. My hand moving up and down their shafts, then down to their balls, rubbing and massaging them.

Then David stepped back and pulled me to my feet. His hand went to my tit, cupping it as he rubbed. Abe worked on my other tit. The feelings that were washing over me were so intense. And when they both lowered their heads to suck on my nipples, I was a goner. Both nipples were being sucked on at the same time, but with different techniques. Amazing!!

As they both played with my tits, we moved to the bed. They lay down, settling me between them. Our arms and legs became a tangle of skin. They had my legs lying across each of them, spreading my pussy wide. They ran their hands down my inner thighs and over the sensitive junction leading to the swell of my pussy lips.

I think at one point they each had a finger in my cunt at the same time. Abe's thick long fingers almost felt like a cock. "Ohhhhhhhh, that was nice." I cooed.

He continued to move one in and out even after David pulled his out.

Abe moved down between my legs and started licking my pussy. He made several long slow licks all the way up my slit. Oh! That was amazing! My pierced clit was sticking out between my pussy lips and each time he did that, his tongue would lightly brush against it, driving me totally insane! I slid my fingers into his hair and pushed his face into me, grinding my pussy against his mouth.

"I"M CUMMMIIINNNGGGG!" I cried.

Then he pushed his fat finger into my cunt and finger fucked me hard and fast. I could see my juices flying all over the place. Then while he sucked my clit he continued to finger fuck me. I had several good hard cums, gushing my juices all over his face.

While Abe was finger fucking me and sucking my clit, David moved up by my face. I was stroking and sucking his cock. He held the back of my head and pulled me up onto it. Fucking my mouth.

I could feel the head of his dick hitting the back of my throat and sometimes pushing into it. My hand reached up under his cock and played with his balls. He was so hard. I think it really turned him on to see another man's head disappearing in between my thighs, licking my pussy.

After I had orgasmed for the umpteenth time, Abe pulled away from me and moved up between my legs. He approached me while stroking his cock. I reached down and wrapped my hand around it. I was still sucking David's cock. I guided Abe's cock into my cunt.

Oh damn, he pushed it into me slowly. I lifted up against him forcing it in deeper. Ohhhh it was so thick! I could feel it spreading me open.

Then he started fucking me, pushing and pulling his cock in and out nice and slow. I was so turned on, I was nearly out of my mind with lust! I wanted to scream "FUCK ME! FUCK ME HARD!" but I couldn't with a mouth full of manjewels. All I could do was moan around it.

Then I heard David say, "OH FUCK SLUT! I'M CUMMING!!"

Great big gobs of thick hot gooey cum shot down my throat as I gulped it down. Then I felt Abe give one big thrust and he was cumming in my hot pussy! That was the most erotic thing I have ever done. My body swallowing up the salty cum of two men! At that point, I think I would have done just about anything they suggested!

Abe collapsed on top of me and David beside me. I could feel cum trickling out of my pussy and running down the corners of my mouth. I was reaching out with my tongue and licking David's cum off my lips.

After a brief break, Abe took my face in his hands and kissed me. That turned me on sooo much. I felt my pussy throbbing at full force once again as we kissed.

Abe's semi hard cock was still resting between my pussy lips. As we kissed, I started moving against him and grinding my clit on his cock. David was lying there, pinching and squeezing my nipples, as he slowly stroked himself.

We dozed off for a while and when we woke up, I was once again in the middle, and I was spooning Abe while David was spooning me. I have never felt anything so nice as that. Wedged in between two hard bodies. Wow! It was awesome!

I started moving my hips slightly. Rubbing my ass against David's cock and my pussy rubbing Abe's ass. I could feel David's cock getting hard as I continued moving against it. He slid his arms around me pulling my ass back against him, and pushing into me.

I moaned softly as Abe turned around and lifted my leg. Then David moved up between them and slid his cock into my pussy from behind.

As David thrust his prick into my pussy, Abe rubbed my clit. "Ohhhhhhh fuckkkk, that drives me crazy!" I moaned.

Then Abe lay down beside me, with his head towards my legs. He continued rubbing my clit and I took his cock into my mouth. I believe every woman should have this experience. It was WILD! David was pussy-pounding!! Abe was massaging my clit! and I was sucking Abe's hard throbbing cock!

I was moving my mouth back and forth on Abe's cock with the same rhythm David was fucking my cunt. Then I saw Abe's head disappear in between my legs. He was flicking his tongue over my hard and swollen clit, as David fucked me. I was moaning around Abe's cock, rapidly sliding it in and out of my mouth. David kept up his pace, while he pinched and pulled at my nipples. Fuckkk, what I was feeling was incredibly hot!

It seemed we all started to cum at once. Abe was the first to let go, spewing his hot cum into my mouth, jet after jet of warm thick gooey delicious cum. He thrust his hips forward, jamming his hard cock down my throat. I swallowed hard, trying to take him all in. Then David grabbed my tits hard and filled my cunt with his hot creamy cum! Abe continued his assault on my clit. Sucking and licking it hard until I came, into his mouth and all over David's cock!

Again, we lay side by side resting for a bit. Then I was on my knees between them, alternately sucking their cocks clean. Licking up and down their shafts and over their balls. Then we lay down and went to sleep. It was a late morning for us.

I was the first to wake. Both cocks were standing straight up! But I figured it wasn't for me, but just because they had to pee. But I played with each of them anyway. I wasn't letting this opportunity pass me by, no way! It didn't take long for them to wake as I moved my hands up and down their stiff cocks.

"Ohhhhhh I gotta piss like a racehorse!" David said with urgency.

We all took turns peeing, and since I was the last to go, I jumped in the shower. Well, imagine my surprise when they both got in with me! The two of them washed me top to bottom, sliding hot soapy water over my swollen pussy lips; I did the same for them. Soaping up their stiff rods. Only one thing feels nicer than a hard slippery wet cock and that's two slippery wet cocks! After we dried off, we went back into the bedroom, hot and horny again, ready for one last session!

Abe had wanted to try something. He lay on his back on the bed, his cock standing straight up once again. He told me to straddle him, lowering my pussy down over his cock, which I did without hesitation!

He made a few pumps into my already wet cunt and pulled me down, pressing my tits against his chest. He then told me to push down on his cock. Raising my ass in the air, which I did. Then David straddled the both of us, lowering himself so his hard cock was pressing against my ass hole; Abe grabbed my ass, pulling my cheeks apart then David slowly slid the head of his well lubed cock into my ass. Ohhhhhhhhhh, I was so full of cock, I was near passing out.

Abe started fucking me, thrusting his hips up and down. As he pushed me up slightly, my ass would ride up on David's cock. Oh fuck! It was incredible!

I was grinding my clit against Abe's pelvis, and it was driving me crazy. I had four hard cums in about twenty minutes. My whole body was trembling and shaking.

The guys continued sliding their cocks into me. It didn't take long for them to cum. Abe spurting his hot cum into my cunt and David pushed his cock into my ass as far as he could as he filled me!

I could feel cum oozing out around both their cocks! Once we calmed down a bit, David pulled out of my ass and collapsed on the bed. I was so weak I couldn't move off Abe. I lay there panting, with his cock deeply embedded in my twitching pussy.

"Ohhhh fuck! that was hot!" Abe said, and David agreed.

I could barely speak above a whisper. "Yesssss," I breathed deeply.

Later that night, David and I were making supper and I started talking about our previous evening... my pussy still soaked from the last 12 hours of hot fun. Tonight I will definitely fuck David's brains out; I will also count the days until something this hot happens again... and get all dripping wet every time I think about it.

Sun-Kissed Surprise

Spring had finally arrived. Jessica had the day to herself because her son was gone to stay at his grandparents' house for the weekend while her hubby was out taking care of some errands. Jessica decided to lie out in the backyard and enjoy the warm sun.

As she lay naked on her stomach, discreetly hidden from any of the neighbors view she could feel the warm rays beating down on her olive-kissed skin. Jessica was feeling very relaxed, several hours had passed in the warm wonderful sun, while her only worry was to lift her head every so often so that she could take a sip of an ice cold Pina colada that she made for herself in a huge insulated mug.

Drifting in and out of brief moments of sleep she was enjoying this wonderful Saturday afternoon without any obligations whatsoever but she'd have to get up soon because her hubby was due home soon so they could go out for dinner.

As she turned over and prepared to get up, she saw her hubby David at the back patio door, he slid it opened and greeted her with a smile "Enjoying the sun I see?" as she acknowledged him and got up to go give him a kiss. "I have a surprise for you" he said to which she looked at him with curiosity. "Put this on" David said as he handed her a blindfold. "What? For real???" Jessica asked as he quickly nodded in confirmation.

Jessica slowly slide the blindfold over her head. "Okay, now what?" she asked with a sarcastically teasing tone. "I'll guide you" David responded as he took her by the shoulders and guided her through the yard. She could feel the soft wisps of grass beneath her feet as she visualized her steps in her head. "Now walk slowly" David said as he guided her feet onto the warm pavement. "Why am I going into the garage???" Jessica asked inquisitively. She could tell where he was leading her, and she was confused.

After she could tell she was inside he tied her hands behind her back and sat her down on a soft surface that felt like a mattress. She heard the garage door closing and then the sound cut out. Jessica was confused "David? What's going on here? I'm not sure I like this" and she could tell that her words were echoing as if she had been placed into a box.

"David? What's going on? Answer me!" Jessica said, her tone growing with concern with her hands still tied. David replied "Don't worry Jessica, just organizing the surprise, you'll like it.... just about ready..." as he untied her hands. She started to feel around and noticed she *was* in a box of some sort, one built with wood. Starting to feel freaked out, she pulled down the blindfold with a quick sense of urgency and her concerns were replaced with surprise.

She couldn't speak for several seconds as she looked around the box. There were several holes in the box and you wouldn't believe what were in these holes... penises! Some were rock hard, some were flaccid but there were several. She was surrounded by four of them! "David?! What... I mean who's are these? None of them are yours!!!" David replied wryly "...and you're not getting out of the box until you've made every one of them cum all over you so I suggest you get to work slut!"

Jessica's pussy was getting drippier at a surprising pace, having cock in her hands and mouth always did this to her. Here she was in a comfortable box, surrounded by such beautiful cocks and she had absolutely no clue whose they were, but she didn't care. Her pussy was burning with desire, but it was going to have to wait, she had work to do, and after all she absolutely *fucking adored* sucking cock!

She looked around and touched each of the cocks, trying to decide who to suck first. It was actually a challenge because even though she had some experience enjoying multiple cocks at once, there was always only two and the scenarios with which she got to enjoy them were for the most part planned and controlled.

She decided to reward the guy that the hardest cock was attached to first as she licked the tip and stroked it with her hand. She could hear a moan from outside the box as she slowly slipped her warm wet lips around the throbbing hard cock. Licking and sucking she could feel it filing up with hot cum as she enjoyed filling her mouth with thick meaty cocks with rock hard definition. She could only imagine the other guys outside the box witnessing her talents by watching his face as he gets sucked by her talented cocksucker mouth. Her hubby David then said "That's a good slut Jessica, take that cock and make it cum all over you. Show these guys what a talented cocksucker you are". Her pussy was dripping down her legs as her excitement rose, knowing these guys were all listening to her warm wet mouth and sexy slurps. She couldn't recognize the moans but she was loving how loud this stud was getting as she sucked with even more determination. She was going to get the seed, she wanted that thick hot cum to splash all over her. She could feel it building up and the moans getting less controlled as she felt the cum stretching up the shaft and she pulled it out of her mouth and jerked it off, gobs and gobs of white cum splashed her hot sexy face and dripped down all over her beautiful big tits.

Her pussy was literally dripping at this point as she felt the warm thick cum slowly dripping down the sides of her cheeks and the bottom of her chin onto her tits as it slowly creeped downward towards her aching mound. She decided to turn 180 degrees to the biggest cock. As she turned she saw how swollen and hard he was, and his cock was huge! She felt it throbbing in her hands, the warmth radiating from his meat was driving her nuts. While she loved sucking cock, the thought of all of these cocks taking turn pounding her was almost torturous. She opened her mouth wide and was happy to see that she was just able to fit the fat piece of cock into her mouth and as the nob slowly slipped over her tongue and into her mouth she heard a loud deep moan, almost like a grunt of surprise as she smiled wryly with the cock in her face. Letting her warm wet saliva drip all up and down the shaft she also used her hands to stroke the rest of the member as she expertly did what she does best, fill her slutty mouth with cock and descend into the recesses of her slutty dirty mind as she increased her pace. Sucking up and down the shaft she massaged his balls and she realized the box she was in was narrow enough for the cocks to touch her shoulders... the two other perverts were rubbing their cocks on her shoulders as she sucked off the third. As usual her hubby was encouraging her to do a good job. She heard him from outside the box "That's a good slut, suck the cum out of that cock bitch" which only made her more eager. At this point the cum from the previous dude was all down her tits and stomach and partially caked on to her face. "What a filthy slut I am" is all she could think as she continued to suck his cock. She couldn't feel the cum that had been oozing down her stomach due to a previous surgery that left nerve endings dull, but she certainly felt it when it reached the top of her pussy mound and continued it's descending trickle. Now her pussy lips were not only wet with her own juices, it was also getting basted in some hot warm sticky man milk and her body started to tighten, she wanted to play with herself so badly! Her sucking and slurping was increasing in speed as she felt the cock swelling up and his body clearly tightening up as he lost control and convulsed moaning loudly and groaning between whatever words he could get out of his throat "Ohhhh fuckk.... sluttt... goddd... fuckkkk.... ooooooohhhh", his thick load of hot cum almost choked her as she took the cock out of her mouth and had the rest explode all over her face, she could feel the mess these guys were making, only two down and her hair face tits and now pussy were caked with hot cum.

As she stopped for a second to take a break and catch her breath she heard her hubby and the other guys talking about what a good cocksucker she was. She also heard her hubby say to the other guys that the cameras were a good idea and at that point she realized that the circles around the box were actually multiple cameras to catch all the action so she could see what a slut she was afterwards. What she didn't realize was that the first guy was not only hard again, but that he was stroking his cock while she was getting off the second guy and watching the second guy cum made him lose his edge. While resting she suddenly felt jets of hot cum hit her back and ass and gush all over her. She didn't even bother to move, it was too late to help, she just let it cover her backside and smiled, now fantasizing at how hot the camera footage would look later.

A mixture of both warm wet dripping cum and sticky drying cum began to cake all over her face and tits while she continued to enjoy the feeling of the cum dripping down over her aching pussy, burning with desire and the cum that splashed down the small of her back had reached her puckering tight asshole. All she could think was what a slut she was as she muttered "I'm such a slut" and the guys outside the box waited eagerly.

She sat at the back of the box with one cock on each side and began to stroke them both, one in each hand. They didn't know it but her hands were covered in hot cum which made the stroking all that more slippery. She could hear two sets of loud moans as she jerked them both off, moving her head back and forth taking turns sucking each cock. Out of the corner of her eye she saw a condom. Either her hubby left it in there or it fell out of one of the guys jean pockets while she was blowing them. She had an idea! She quietly opened it up and carefully slipped it onto one of the cocks while continuing to stroke him. She quickly got on all fours and held his cock and guided it into her pussy. "Oh gawwwdddd" was all she could say as she finally felt a rock hard throbbing cock inside her with the other one bobbing in her face she grabbed hold and put it in her mouth. "Mmmmhhmmm" is all she could muffle as she was getting pounded from behind, mashing her cunt back against the side of the box as he buried himself balls deep in her sweet honey pot and she could taste the warm precum oozing out of the other cock she was expertly sucking. Back and forth she was enjoying the motion, feeling that cock push the cum that had oozed down her pussy and ass being pushed deeper and deeper into her dirty box. The irony was she used a condom but couldn't help that the other cum had gushed down there. She was getting closer as the balls were mashing against her clit as she was getting fucked real hard. The friction was making her body shake as she focused on her own pleasure like a horny little slut and then she exploded hard! Her pussy quivered, her moans filled the garage, the box only containing a bit of the volume as the slut lost control of herself. As she finished cumming she felt the cock pull out of her and then plunged deep back in her as the moans turned loud and faster and he came deep in her wet aching pussy. Jet after jet of gooey cum splashing her inner walls and she started a second wave of cumming as she realized he pulled out only to remove the condom and fill her up with cum. As her orgasm finished she felt a load of hot sticky cum exploding all in her mouth as she greedily swallowed it back figuring she's already been filled with so many loads, if it wasn't safe her man would have stopped her a long time ago, he must have had them tested.

She collapsed in the box and rested, panting for her breath, covered in hot cum and lay there like a hot well used slut, aching to feel her man next, but exhausted from already being used like the slut she was.

Cucked By Wife: Voyeur Hotwife Humiliation Cleanup

Trevor Cox stood by the front door waiting impatiently for his hotwife's return. He was feeling somewhat cold in his pink ruffled panties, a frilly grey apron, and a pair of colorful palm shoes. Apart from his steel chastity cage and some red lipstick, he wore nothing else. His hotwife, Vanessa, had called around 45 minutes prior to inform him that she was en route home and that she was being escorted by two special guests. When Vanessa told Trevor that she was bringing visitors, he was immediately on his feet to make the required arrangements.

Vanessa had been cuckolding Trevor from the initial days of their female-led marriage. Trevor, aged around fifteen years older than her, was short, bald and paunchy and had a little penis. Vanessa, on the other hand, was energetic, had a great body, a beautiful face and would be considered by most men to be supermodel material.

Only 34 years of age, Vanessa had beautiful wavy long blonde hair, crystal blue eyes, a cover girl's face and luscious, plump lips that were some of the most kissable lips anyone could have ever seen. Her body was just as incredible; busty natural breasts which were almost too large for such a petite woman; swelled opulently from her fine-boned chest. Resembling the size of melons, the valley of her mounds were a tantalizing sight for any male. Her sensitive nipples, easily hardened by the faintest friction of fabric of her clothes, poked through nearly every shirt that she owned. Her slim waist and perfectly toned tummy streamed easily down to wide flaring hips that led to long, smooth thighs and outstandingly shaped hemispherical scooped butt cheeks. With a tempting hourglass figure, she was the subject of envy for many of the neighborhood ladies and an attractive distraction to nearly all of the men.

They complemented very well as a couple. They loved to watch the same TV shows and movie genres, and they enjoyed listening to the same music. They shared similar political perspectives and cherished spending numerous hours discussing stimulating and provocative topics. Most importantly, they loved spending time with each other. But they had a twisted side to their relationship. While Vanessa was a top sales executive in a reputable fashion brand apparel company, Trevor stayed at home and performed all of the household chores. If Vanessa would go shopping, Trevor would look after the house as if he were a nanny, and take care of the cleaning, cooking, laundry and whatever other duties were required.

Their sexual life was very unusual. Vanessa admired and adored enormous, Herculean, hunk men. They were the only breed of men whom she preferred and loved to engage in sexual relations with. In their seven-year relationship, Trevor had engaged in sexual relations with her just twice, on their honeymoon in Hawaii and five years ago on their second anniversary. But in some way or the other, he was lucky enough to be involved in her thrilling erotic adventures. When she would bring any of her lovers home, his indispensable duty was to become their obedient domestic servant. This also included degrading tasks such as assuming the role of fluffer, cum cleaner, or whatever else they wanted him to be. Being most intimately associated with her extraordinary sexual adventures was highly exciting for him and he always looked forward to these sensational encounters.

When Vanessa called him a half an hour prior, Trevor had been relaxing after his household chores. As a result of the call, he had a series of daunting tasks to perform. After undressing and sliding himself into his special garments, he put a set of fresh sheets and a new comforter onto the bed. He sprayed scented air fresheners around the house and then went to the kitchen and arranged some mouth-watering appetizers. He placed champagne on ice, dimmed the lights and tuned the radio to some sensual jazz music. He turned on the oven and started roasting some vegetables. He was almost done garnishing the delectable starters and the dishes when he heard the cars parking in the garage. His heart raced with the anticipation of another stirring adventure and his little dicklet twitched in his cage envisioning his hotwife's wild moans in her lovers' arms. Trevor ran and stood by the front doorway.

Their cheerful voices resonated in Trevor's ears from the outside and soon the door opened. Vanessa entered first, followed by two tall and handsome Herculean hunks. Whenever Trevor saw his hotwife, Vanessa, he would be immediately mesmerized by her hypnotic charm and grace. She looked stunning. As soon as she turned her back toward him, he took her jacket, one of the many rituals in which Trevor was trained successfully.

"Peanut, this is Mr. Shane Marshall and Mr. Luke Garner. I expect you'll be a good boy and ensure they feel at home," Vanessa asserted. Turning on her heels, she spoke to her studs, "Shane, Luke... My husband Trevor is here to take care of our needs and desires. He loves to be summoned by his pet name, peanut. Without any question or doubt, he'll literally do anything you ask of him. He'll set up our dinner and drinks, he'll sing, he'll dance, he'll even suck your cock hard for me. He'll even go so far as to wipe your ass clean if he's required. He is our slave for tonight."

'Suck your cock hard for me.' Those words sent chills down his spine and for a moment, Trevor felt his heart in his throat. He was leaking from his caged dicklet at that very tempting thought.

Vanessa continued, "If you command him to wash your cars, he'll do that in his panties, no questions asked. He'll even polish your shoes if you tell him to. So, don't be shy. Besides, he has a habit of being grumpy at times if you don't ask him to do any demeaning chores. So, take advantage!" She left the men to head to her room so that she could freshen up.

"I have a very sexy hotwife. I like watching her get fucked by these studs. She definitely has the pick of the litter, doesn't she? Imagine how sexy it will be to see her lie back and spread her legs while they take care of her... I'll watch their long hard cocks stretch her married little hole, thrusting hard, pounding vigorously as they take her, their thick meat penetrating deep inside of her." As Trevor thought about these wild thoughts, he felt a tingle. He couldn't help but think about all of the naughty possibilities and lustful events that were about to happen.

“Mr. Marshall, Mr. Garner,” Trevor stated, “Please allow me to take your jacket. There is champagne on ice, but feel free to tell me if you would like anything else. Also, please feel free to ask for anything else in order to make your evening with my hotwife most delightful and entertaining. It’s my duty.” He curtsied.

“Thanks, peanut! I’d love some champagne. What about you, Luke?” Shane asked Luke.

“Yeah! Champagne for me too!” Luke snickered.

Trevor opened the champagne and poured them each a glass. He also placed some nuts and berries out for snacks. When they had been served, he diverted his attention back to the kitchen once again.

Having the expertise of a chef, he prepared the dinner table with palatable dishes consisting of chicken fricassee, cheesy croissant casserole, and vegetable salads. In the meantime, Vanessa returned and joined Luke and Shane on the couch. As she settled between her hunky studs, they got busy planning for the upcoming weekend vacation. It appeared that the group had a mutual love for the Caribbean. Vanessa had already been there with Trevor a couple of years back. Undoubtedly, her erotic Jamaican adventurous holiday was still fresh in her memories. She was dripping wet just knowing that she was about to fuck and suck those two Herculean studs that night. And her wild memories just catalyzed these arousals.

As for Luke and Shane, they kept on playing with her hair which outlined her areolas over her top. As she wasn't wearing any bra, her nipples protruded through the fabric, showing prominently through her blouse. Shane, from time to time delicately caressed her back, provoking even more impure thoughts in her mind. When Trevor peeked in, he noticed their pants straining beneath their growing bulges. Clearly, they were enjoying their time with his sexy hotwife. There was a lot of laughter and flirting resonating from the sofa. He couldn't wait to see his hotwife fulfilling her savage lust with her studs.

Trevor refilled their glasses and arranged the delectable dishes on the table. He noticed that the talking had waned and Vanessa was kissing Shane passionately. Luke was playing with her voluptuous breasts through her top while her hands were busy exploring the strained bulges in both of their jeans.

"Shall I set up the room?" Trevor quietly asked Vanessa.

She grinned and nodded her approval between kisses.

Trevor went to his hotwife's room and lit a few candles, as he turned on some dim lighting. He restraightened the bedsheets, spread some rose petals upon it, and adjusted the volume of the music coming from the speakers. He arranged a pitcher of cool water and three glasses on the bedside table. Finally, he placed out various lubes that matched Vanessa's preference. With a quick spray of the room air freshener, the environment was ready for his hotwife's upcoming lustful and wild adventure.

The entire time, the cuckold husband's mind was in a frenzy, consumed with lustful thoughts about his hotwife feeling her studs' while they ravaged her body. His caged shaft was leaking, his fingers were cold and his heart was beating rapidly. His legs were getting weaker with every passing moment. The cuckold husband mustered all of his strengths and returned to the living room, informing his hotwife and guests, "Your bed is ready."

The hotwife's eyes glittered as she freed herself from her studs' arms and smiled with delight, "My husband just prepared the room for us to have sex in, isn't he such a good boy? He always gets hard watching me with other men. What a good little cucky" Trevor's heart skipped a beat at his hotwife's comments. He was unsure whether it was praise or humiliation. But, the way his cuckold mind reacted to her words, the way his hard dicklet throbbed in his cage and the way goosebumps coursed over his skin, he was a slave of his own perverted desire.

Vanessa got up from the couch and led the way to her room. Trevor strolled behind them, rolling a cart that carried their champagne glasses and the ice bucket with the half-empty champagne bottle. Along the way, Luke and Shane didn't miss any opportunity, as they continued to explore Vanessa's seductive body. They caressed her sensuous curves and smacked her fleshy ass playfully; he was enjoying the view from behind. The resonance from the impact of the ass smack was felt in the cuck husband's heart and his leaking dick. In the room, Vanessa let herself fall in her lovers' arms and took turns kissing them passionately. The way that Shane turned her towards the cuck husband as he stuck his tongue in the hotwife's throat, made it abundantly clear that he was the one in charge. Vanessa gazed back at her cuck hubby as she returned the favor with her tongue. Her icy blue eyes were enough to encourage Trevor in doing what he needed to do in order to help Luke who was fumbling with his pants.

"Sir, might you want to use the bathroom now to avoid any future interruptions?" Trevor inquired.

"Indeed, peanut, where is it?" Luke answered enthusiastically.

"Please follow me, Sir," Trevor replied with pure politeness.

Luke followed Trevor towards the bathroom. Trevor's heart was beating like a thousand drums, thinking about what he was going to do. He swallowed hard. Kneeling down beside the toilet he stood before the toilet and reached for the hunk's zipper.

Trevor unzipped him and reached inside. He pulled out a wonderful huge penis that Vanessa would undoubtedly love. He held it and pointed it towards the toilet. Luke shivered at the feeling of cuck hubby's cold fingers on his shaft. The cuck husband felt it swell somewhat just before the excretion came spurting out from the urethra. A mighty stream followed and sprayed relentlessly from it. When it stopped, the cuck husband gave it a shake and licked off the final drops from the tip. He then reached for a warm wipe and cleaned it.

"Would you like me to clean up your scrotum and your butt, Mr. Garner?"

"You know, peanut, I must say, no one has ever asked me that favor. Definitely, go ahead," he replied cautiously.

Trevor unfastened his belt and pants and brought them down. He cleaned his scrotum and the crack of his butt first with his tongue, followed by a warm baby wipe. The cuck hubby shivered as his nostrils inhaled the pungent, sweaty aroma while his tongue curled from the bitterness. Luke shivered with feverish excitement as he felt the cuck husband's servile lips cleaning his scrotum. Once the cuck was done, he pulled Trevor's briefs and pants back up, zipped up his pants and buckled his belt. Trevor handed Luke a toothbrush with toothpaste on it and patiently waited while he used it to clean his mouth. Soon, Luke was done and Trevor gave him a glass of water.

"Mr. Garner, Sir, your cock is superb. It's so big and thick," Trevor praised. "Have you had the delight of fucking my hotwife yet? Or will this be your first experience with her?"

"Thank you for the compliment, peanut. This will, in fact, be my first time fucking your hotwife, but it won't be the last," Luke chuckled. Trevor felt chills down his spine as soon as he heard his demeaning comments. His caged dicklet throbbed at the very enticing thought. He gulped and moved his eyes downward.

"Indeed, Sir, if you allow me, just a note of advice to a real man, my hotwife likes it rough and hard. Actually she loves it. She will be exceptionally aroused if you pull her hair and choke her as you fuck her," Trevor gulped.

Trevor escorted Luke back to the bedroom. Shane's hands were rapidly caressing up on Vanessa's succulent breasts, tracing and measuring their shape. Delicate and soft touches were increasing her arousal. Shane's mouth, within no time, was drooling to participate in the sexual ecstasy, planted kisses on her glowing skin before venturing into her luscious lips. His kisses were so captivating and were such a manly mark of him. Vanessa always had a spark of intuition where she could tell about a man's love-making skills from his kissing technique.

"Hey guys, this is so unfair," Luke chuckled and intervened.

"Fuck man! This bitch is hot, couldn't wait!" Shane countered.

"Hey, Luke! Was peanut good to you?" Vanessa teased.

"Oh! He was excellent. Nobody ever did to me what he did for me." Luke grinned.

"That's making me jealous!" Shane replied.

"Oh! Don't worry Shane. He would do the same for you as well. Thanks, peanut for taking care of my guests." Vanessa smiled. "I always tell him it's not gay if he does it for me."

Vanessa's demeaning tone rocked Trevor's senses and smashed his pride into the ground. As they laughed out loud at her ridicule, his caged dicklet pulsated and leaked even more. He inquired as to whether her studs were ready to be undressed before he ventured into the kitchen to set up the plates.

The hunks nodded their approval and he dropped to his knees. He loosened their shoes and slipped them off. He reached under their pant legs to the top of their socks and dragged them off too. He rose up on his legs and pulled their shirts out of their pants and then began to unbutton them. One by one, Trevor unbuttoned both of the men's shirts and then slipped them off and then hung them in his hotwife's closet. Coming back to his knees, he gradually opened their pants and brought them down to the ground, waiting for each hunk stud to step out of them so that he could fold them and place them neatly aside. Left with only their boxers, he pulled them down and revealed their surprise packages to his hotwife.

On his knees, before the studs, Trevor gazed upward at them and asked, "Sirs, please allow me to use my mouth to give your penises a full erection?"

Shane and Luke nodded their approval, both with wicked grins, Trevor carried his lips to Shane's half-erect shaft and started to kiss his way to the head. He opened his mouth wide, then wider, and took him all in. Soon it was hardening in his servile mouth. When it gained its full length, the cuck husband's jaw was stretched out as far as it could be. He inhaled the musky scent which fueled the excitement in the cuckold's perverted mind. Soon, Shane's cock was hard as steel in the cuck hubby's mouth. The cuck husband started to bob his head back and forth and just when he had gained a rhythmic pace, he heard Vanessa's voice.

"Don't get carried away, peanut. Your job is to get him hard and not suck him off," Vanessa rebuked.

"Right," said Luke looking down at the spluttering husband, "Now it's my turn!"

Luke rammed his cock into the cuck hubby's mouth. The invading cock felt flaccid in the beginning, but within moments, it was huge in his mouth, poking violently at the back of his throat. "MMMPPHHHFFF!!!" Trevor gagged as he choked on this huge piece of fuck meat. The cuck hubby couldn't breathe and started to feel his lungs burning as the bull enjoyed his tight throat. The hunk man pulled out and let the cuck husband cough and splutter on the floor. Trevor was gasping for air and panting hard. "I think he liked that," Luke snickered to Vanessa, who was now in a lustful state.

"Is that what you want Sissy? You wanna be Daddies' cocksucker in panties, don't you?"

Vanessa teased. Trevor nodded his acknowledgment.

Trevor felt aroused at the abuse that he was receiving. "You slut boy cock-sucking sissy! You've no idea how much I love using your soft puffy lips; I bet they're just like your hotwife's cunt." Shane ridiculed, as he was consumed with both wild pleasure and savage lust. Every time he pushed his cock in, Trevor's face slammed into his sweaty pubes and the musky aroma filled his nostrils.

Vanessa was a sex Goddess. Her thick, dense, and blonde hair dangled around and encircled her beautiful face perfectly. Her icy blue eyes gazed enthusiastically at the lewd adventures that she was about to receive. Her beautiful lips were swollen and eager, crashing against her lovers' lips, chests, and cocks. She wore elegant pink panties and a short silk robe.

Turning to her cuck hubby, she revealed, "You guys have no idea, he's such a true cum slut, if I don't stop him, he'll have all my studs cumming even before I had even gotten to suck them."

"You will get a lot of cum soon enough. But for now, leave us alone and go get the plates ready for dinner."

"Sure, dear," Trevor answered and left the room.

He occupied himself in the kitchen and set up the dinner table perfectly; arranging the plates, cutlery and napkins. He carefully arranged the food upon the table. Everything was so perfect; he felt pride in his own artistic work. Finally he opened a bottle of wine and filled the glasses as he heard his hotwife's groans getting more and more intense from the other room. Not being able to resist himself, he found himself returning back to the entrance of the bedroom door. There she was, his hotwife completely naked with her lovers exploring the delightful ecstasies of the high heavens.

The delicate kissing had long given way and now Luke was straddling Vanessa; his hard throbbing cock was pounding her repeatedly. Vanessa was moaning through his steady thrusts while his strong hands sensuously caressed her seductive body. He was in charge, fucking her in front of her cuck husband, and she cherished how savagely he was owning her as his balls slapped against her ass with each thrust of his pounding manhood. Vanessa was consumed by her arousal, lust glimmered in her eyes, as Luke owned her body. Luke pulled out and flipped Vanessa over; looking over at the cuck husband and laughed as he plunged his hard cock back inside her. On all fours, Vanessa moaned loudly as Luke fucked her like the bitch in heat that she was; and he was enjoying making the cuck watch.

Shane couldn't believe his eyes as he witnessed Vanessa's body losing control as she shuddered on Luke's cock, her whole body convulsed as she came around his shaft, causing her nectar to spew out and down his legs. Shane had his fair share of experience with women, most of them were models and escorts, but none of them matched Vanessa's sex appeal. He waited for his turn and watched while Luke continued to ravish the wild beauty on the bed. Luke reached to the nightside table and grabbed a blindfold, tossing it towards Vanessa. Eagerly, she slipped it over her eyes. Vanessa always had a thing for blindfolds, not being able to see heightened her senses and made everything more arousing. Luke flipped her over onto her back and began to kiss her soft skin. Warm, moist kisses traced lines on her glowing skin and now the entirety of her senses focused on his lips. Without knowing where his lips would venture to next, each touch turned out to be increasingly and exceptionally electric; her skin reacted to every sensual contact.

All over her body, Vanessa felt his touch, every nerve ending shivered, sending electric pulses to her brain. The ache within her pussy escalated to new heights. Vanessa loved the thrilling sensations from the unknown touches, and the inability to prepare herself for whatever would come next.

Trevor gulped as he watched Luke steer his hypnotic gaze from her body onto her pussy lips and settle his mouth upon her crotch. Vanessa could feel his hot breath on her and she tensed up, in anticipation of what would happen next. Trevor was speechless, watching as Luke slowly licked at her swollen pink pussy lips and his tongue flicked at her swollen hardened clit.

Vanessa's legs bucked with arousal as Trevor suckled on her clit. Jolts of pleasure surged through her body has his tongue flicked her creamy clit. Thick clear fluid dribbled from her pussy down to her asshole. The new, unfamiliar tongue felt amazing and caused her moans to reach heights that Trevor couldn't recall ever hearing before. Luke pushed her legs back further, spreading her wide open before him. He slowly lowered his face downward and she gasped as his tongue touched her puckered asshole. She was in a state of euphoria as he slowly slid his tongue around the edge and pushed it into her tight little backdoor. She felt his tongue slide in and out several motions and then his licks travelled their way back upwards to refocus his attention once again on her pussy. Vanessa clenched her hands on the bedsheets as his tongue penetrated her; she could swear it was as big as her cuck hubby's penis. He fucked her hole with his tongue multiple times before proceeding upwards, licking along her swollen lips and then nibbling on her aching clit. The excitement within her was growing exponentially and the occasional delays between teasing licks were driving her into a frenzy.

Luke gazed up at the wild-eyed woman and said, “Do you like having your pussy eaten?”

“Yes, I love it,” Vanessa gasped. “Eat my pussy.”

Luke attacked her overflowing pussy fast, rapidly running his tongue along her slit, from her asshole to her clit. Her body convulsed in response to the exquisite skills of his talented tongue. She was rhythmically raising her hips as if she was imagining herself getting fucked. Luke heard the slut hotwife moaning loudly beneath his talented tongue. Her moans escaped from the back of her throat as he scoured his tongue all around her throbbing, leaking married pussy.

Vanessa’s breathing became shallow and erratic. She gasped for air, her body tightened and then convulsed in wild lust as he lapped rhythmically at her clit. “Ohh! Ohh! My god,” she screamed. Vanessa unclenched her fists from the bedsheet and grabbed the back of Luke’s head, mashing his face into her yearning pussy and held him tight. His long meaty tongue continued to lap at her clit with steady rhythm as her body began to convulse. She raised her hips to match her lover’s tongue onslaughts. Vanessa felt her pussy spasming as she screamed out loud with ecstasy, "I'm cuuummminng."

She collapsed back onto the bed feeling sensationally relieved. Her panting was erratic and arrhythmic, as she struggled to catch her breath. "Oh my god," she moaned. She continued gasping vigorously as Luke continued to eat her married pussy, claiming it, conquering it, marking it as his. Her body continued to involuntarily buck with each onslaught of his tongue. Right on the heels of the first climax, her body tensed up again and she exploded; jet after jet of thick warm nectar spewed from her pussy; like an endless fountain, spraying everywhere. Nothing was safe; not Luke, not the bed, not even the floor. Her nectar was everywhere. Vanessa's body went limp from exhausted as Luke raised his face with a grin.

Shane was tired of watching. He strolled over to Vanessa, his enormous cock throbbing with anticipation, leading the way. Luke removed the blindfold from her eyes. Vanessa was all the while descending from her climax when she saw Shane standing at the side of her bed. She had overlooked him. She felt somewhat embarrassed at putting on live porno for a man she had just known for two or three hours. But it immediately faded away when she saw his monstrous cock awaiting its chance to invade the pit of her womanhood. His cock was really marvelous. It stood out from his groin measuring around eleven inches with a thickness equaling her wrist. A huge pulsating blue vein ran down the underside of his throbbing pole. "I bet God, even doesn't have a cock of that magnitude," she wondered; corrupted in her overpowering lust.

"Bitch, let me show you what I'm capable of. I know you need this." Luke pulled her hips up, fingered her moistened married pussy just to sense the amount of lubrication her overpowering climax had caused and invaded her married pussy with the dome-sized head of his enormous fuck meat. Vanessa groaned. "Oh! YES, baby! Show my husband how to fuck like a real man". Those words provoked his excitement to new heights and he pushed his cock almost halfway into her married sacred hole. "Vanessa, I realize your cuck doesn't satisfy you. A magnificent young lady like you deserves all the pleasures that he can't give you. I'm fucking you for you." Luke shoved another two inches in. Vanessa was lost in how good his cock felt as he penetrated deeper inside her married womanhood. She pushed her body downwards against his enormous fuck pole, and soon her pussy had engulfed his erection up to his balls. She had never felt anything so deep inside of her before. The feeling of truly being full triggered her orgasm and sent her over the edge. Her body tightened up and began to convulse as a climax erupted from deep within her. Wave after wave, her pussy clenched him as it gushed down his shaft.

"Oh, my God, Luke. I love your huge cock. Fuck me! Make me feel like a woman again! Don't stop until you fill me with your thick hot cum!" Vanessa screamed in ecstasy. As Luke fucked Vanessa, Shane, already hard, put his cock inside her mouth. Obediently, she sucked his shaft as her moans vibrated around it.

Trevor stood frozen in sheer lust as he watched his married hotwife slurping on Shane's big cock while getting fucked by Luke. He stood there right at the threshold of the door, watching his hotwife breaking the vows of marriage like she had so many times before. For a moment, Vanessa stared at the doorway. She could see his dark shadowy figure in the dimness of the environment. She always enjoyed being watched while having sex. Trevor felt incredibly aroused, his face was contorted as he investigated her eyes in the candlelight. He found it hard to breathe. His mind was in a conflicted fusion of painful humiliation and electrifying excitement.

Shane pulled his cock out of her mouth and smacked her face with it. "Try and deep throat it, bitch," he commanded. Vanessa trembled with feverish excitement at his abruptness. "I'm sure no woman would ever feel anything in her pussy after taking that enormous fuck pole," she thought internally as it swayed enchantingly before her, captivating her lustful thoughts. Vanessa reached out with her tongue and licked the tip. She then began to plant little kisses all around the bulbous head. She found it difficult to focus on her slurping as Luke pounded her pussy. Vanessa licked down the underside of his enormous shaft and licked his apple-sized balls, first the left then the right. Then, she measured the length with her tongue and lips and took his whole cock head into her mouth. Shane was a Greek god and deserved to be worshipped by the sex goddess, Vanessa, and she was doing her best to satisfy him.

"I told you to deep throat it, bitch, not kiss it." Shane grabbed the back of her head and fiercely forced his cock into her mouth as much as she could take in.

She groaned around his giant cock as another climax erupted from the depths of her married pussy. When Shane let go of her head and removed his hands, she worked towards deep-throating him without any encouragement required. She pushed against her gag reflex, in an attempt to guide it down her throat. It took minutes of effort, but she kept relentlessly trying until his shaft breached the barrier in her throat. "That is it slut, now you're doing me right." Shane groaned and started fucking her face. She felt so proud that she could pleasure a man giving him such profound pleasure. Her pride only encouraged her even more to prove her oral skills.

Luke was thrusting her married pussy harder and faster than before, he was gasping and his rhythm became erratic. “I’m getting close, slut.” Vanessa took her mouth off Shane’s cock and asserted, “Do it, baby, fill my pussy with your cum. I need to feed my cuck.” Luke shivered at her insanely exciting words and moaned as his cock detonated inside her. The hot thick cum erupted deep inside of her pussy like a hose as she screamed in pleasure; her biggest orgasm of the night overtook her and her body convulsed uncontrollably as her nectar sprayed violently from her pussy. Luke pulled his monster out and she felt so incredibly empty without him in her. His cum spilled from her married pussy and formed a pool on the bed sheet beneath her. “Oh God, this man can cum,” she thought. The load was colossal.

Vanessa turned her attention towards Shane’s yearning cock, glistening before her, coated with her saliva. She deep-throated him once more proving her exceptional oral skills, bobbing her head for minutes, until, with a bestial howl, he shot his hot thick spunk into her mouth. Thick, warm jets of cum filled her mouth, coated her tongue and dribbled down her chin and on to the bed sheet. When she removed her mouth to swallow the precious juice, a subsequent stream erupted from his cock, splashing onto her forehead and cheek. She was shocked at how delicious it tasted and how incredible it felt giving this remarkable hunk such an explosive orgasm.

Trevor was excited at what he was witnessing. He was frozen in a mixture of lust and ridicule.

Vanessa was utterly surprised to see Shane's erection still throbbing hard. His eleven-inch beast was still achingly hard, its huge bulbous head pointing at her.

"It seems that its remaining hard and needs some more action," Shane stated, caressing Vanessa's naked back. Vanessa sat up. His mammoth erection had regained its hardness and full length now and her hand was stroking it. She gazed at it; she licked her parched lips as she prepared to suck him once more. "No bitch; I want to fuck you, I want you to feel this inside of you," he moaned.

Trevor's cock twitched once again as he witnessed his hotwife getting conquered by not one, but two more potent men. Vanessa's pussy let out another little squirt. Her body clearly loved the attention she was receiving, and her mind was completely lost in the desire for the enormous dark shaft in her grasp. She leaned down, drawing her mouth closer to his delightful, veiny shaft.

"Slide your pussy on my cock," Shane commanded. He was going to claim his prize.

“Please be careful, Shane. My husband is not even a third of the length of this cock,” Vanessa looked at the monstrous cock in her grasp. She truly wanted to suck it once more; however, Shane’s recommendation lured her. Vanessa sucked her lower lip in eagerness to feel his hot shaft throbbing between her legs. She straddled his waist and brought herself down onto his pole. Her dripping pussy lips spread out around the base of his erection oozing her lustful excitement and drenching his hardened shaft. She drove her groin down, groaning as she felt his hot and fully erect huge cock throbbing with life inside of her.

Trevor leaned against the wall as his legs weakened, incapable of moving even an inch. “This blend of excitement and humiliation is my dream come true, my most desired fantasy,” he thought. “The acknowledgment that your hotwife needs another man is so exciting. The other man fucking her is making her scream in ecstasy and moaning in profound joy.” Trevor pondered. He felt wave after wave of excitement and envy increasing with each of Shane’s thrusts into his hotwife’s pussy. His pin dick was hard within its cage. The loud moans of his hotwife were driving him wild.

Vanessa slid up and down the base of his erection, increasing her speed. “YES!” she groaned as his hips slapped her bubble butt. Her ass shook rhythmically as she worked her pussy along the entire length of his mammoth erection. In the dimly lit room, Trevor watched in disbelief as he witnessed the big cock disappearing into his hotwife's married cunt, conquering her, claiming her and abusing her very hole which he once proudly owned.

Vanessa had never experienced her nipples being so hard. They stood out at least a half-inch longer than they ever had before. Her areolas were swollen also, causing the ends of nipples to stick out an additional inch longer than ever before. Shane's arms were under his head, eyes shut, with a marvelous look all over. He groaned, raising his hips towards her, lazily opening his eyes and enjoying the delightful view of her ass dancing rhythmically in front of his face with every thrust. Shane reached around and squeezed both of her nipples, waves of profound blissful joy rippled through her body as a result of his touch.

Behaving like the slut that she never was for him, Trevor couldn't believe it when Vanessa begged Shane to fuck her tight hole! She was reacting as if she was possessed by a demon. As a matter of fact, she was possessed by the demon of her own buried lust. Trevor watched in awe as this huge muscled man kissed his hotwife! She ran her delicate hands all over his chiseled body as his huge cock penetrated her deeper than he ever could.

"It's time to mark you as my bitch," Shane whispered. Vanessa looked absolutely puzzled.

"I'll leave my mark on you so that when you see them you will remember who made them," he groaned and dug his teeth deep with full force on her delicate luscious nipple.

"AHHH... OHHHH... AHHHH." Vanessa screamed in an ecstatic blend of pain and pleasure.

Her eyes spread wide and she pushed him back desperately grabbing his hair. But his strong teeth dug deep into the flesh of her succulent nipple and didn't budge. A sharp pain rushed through her body, a tingling flooded through her spine. Goosebumps rolled across her glowing skin. Vanessa bucked in agony, but Shane continued sucking with his teeth dug deeper into her flesh. Within moments, her body somewhat acclimated to the pain and a deep sensation of pleasure surged through her body. The pleasure intensified the sensitivity within her married pussy and triggered her to orgasm. She bucked uncontrollably as she came, as she held his head strongly against her breast, craving him more than ever before.

"Now, I'm going to mark the other tit," Shane groaned, taking the succulent boob in his mouth.

"Ummm... AHHH..." Vanessa felt another orgasm developing deep inside her married pussy. Vanessa groaned louder than before as Shane placed his mouth over her right breast.

“AHHHH... OHHH... MY... FUCKING .... GOD,” Vanessa screamed aloud as if being exorcised. She gasped heavily to endure the pain waiting for it to subside, as the sensation shot electric surges through her body.

Vanessa worked her hips harder and faster, sliding along the entire length of his big cock. She looked down between her breasts and watched his long, wet mammoth shaft sliding in and out of her pussy. This Herculean man’s enormous pole delivered more precum than her husband’s entire cumload, a few times over; however, it would require a great deal of cum to coat such an immense weapon. As she gazed down, big thick gobs of precum oozed from the head of his cock. Her married cunt was milking his big cock real good.

Her pussy was sliding up closer to the head now, and she began concentrating on the end of his shaft over the base of his pole. Her pussy lips spread out around the head and Vanessa’s body shook with desire when another stream of his precum dribbled out. Vanessa whimpered in desire, feeling the head half lodged at the passage to her pussy. All she needed to do was push down and back and his shaft would be inside her. Vanessa was nearing her orgasm again, as she struggled to control her pace.

Vanessa propelled herself up off the pole, his cock head bounced against her sensitive clit. She was losing control as it rubbed against her feverish button. Shane sat up and sucked one of her engorged nipples between his lips. That was all it took to topple her off the peak of excitement. "I'M CUMMING AGAIN!" Vanessa's moans filled the room and quickly escalated into euphoric screams of ecstasy as she lost control of her body and orgasmed again.

Floods of liquid splashed down upon his cock head and ran down his pole. The additional lubrication coupled with her spasming cunt sank her pussy down along his erection and the head pushed inside her. Vanessa's moans continued with deafening consistency.

The Hercules was mauling both her breasts together and kneading both her nipples. He was more of an expert than her pimp husband. He was making Vanessa lose her mind with wild lust. Shane ceased his ministrations for a moment and stated, "It's so hot and wet!" He gazed at Vanessa in wonder. He clipped his lips back over a nipple and sucked, kneading hard with his teeth almost to the point of chewing, crushing her breasts simultaneously.

Vanessa felt as if she was losing her virginity once more. Vanessa pushed back on his chest and gazed at him in the eyes and she gradually plunked down in his lap. “Yes, bitch” Shane gasped, feeling the electric stimulations of being wrapped by her velvet pussy as the entirety of his big cock was covered by her warmth and wetness.

“Oh, Shane, you’re stretching me so good!” Vanessa moaned, overpowered in ecstasy. Vanessa had never felt anything so great. The immense cock head felt like it had pushed into her belly and she could feel its precum dribbling out of her. She couldn’t move. Vanessa just sat in his lap, trembling and shaking. Her vaginal muscles were pressing and twitching all over his thick erection. “I’m going to cum once more.” She focused on the feeling as an intense climax developed in power, her pussy muscles shuddered over every last trace of his mammoth pole.

“Your hot pussy’s draining my cock, bitch,” Shane snorted. His hips bucked as though he was desperate for her movements. “Going to cum!” he moaned. And Shane blasted in her pussy, nearly a minute of convulsions and jets filled her to the brim.

“Come here, peanut!” Vanessa teased. “Did you like watching your hotwife getting fucked? Now it’s time to clean me off. Oh my God! Look at this mess! Clean me up cucky boy!”

Trevor immediately licked the warm gooey cum loads out of her. Licking and slurping, he worked diligently to clean it all up. She grinned and held out her hand with the chastity keys but didn't hand it to him. "Now clean up the puddles on the bed, cucky boy!" He lowered his face and licked the cum from the sheets and slowly gulped it back.

Vanessa gave him a little peck on the cheek and asked her lovers to join them for dinner. Trevor watched her lovers getting dressed and head toward the dinner table. Vanessa teased with a devious chuckle, "So did you enjoy watching your hotwife fuck two real studs?"

Before Trevor could respond, she guided his eyes to the spots of her love bits on her succulent breasts. His yearning eyes followed the indications and all of a sudden he began to tremble as he saw the bite marks on her breasts.

"This...this," he was shaking. Vanessa chuckled and freed him of her chastity and gently patted his cock, which was throbbing hard and aching for a release.

"He always leaves a mark on his sluts. You know, I'm his favorite now," Vanessa answered passionately and grabbed her cuck's pin dick, "Kiss the bruises and say you love me."

“I love you, Vanessa,” Trevor shivered as he lowered his lips to her tits and began to kiss her bruise marks, carefully one by one.

While he kissed them, he reached down and vigorously stroked his uncaged dick. It didn’t take long, his hyper-sensitive, excited little pin dick ejaculated a load into his other hand and onto the floor.

He heard her lovers laugh from the other room as they said, “That bitch is hot! Cucky boy dicklet didn’t even get to fuck her. More fun for the bulls.” He knew what his role was, and he accepted it; he was a cuck.

My Husband & The Gang Fill Me to the Brim

It was a long day, I had just spent several hours helping my sister prepare goodies for an upcoming Christmas celebration. My son was staying at my parents that night so I was anxious to get home to a night of relaxation with my husband, Brian. My mind wandered about the day and I thought about all of the "little stuff" like what I would make for dinner. The drive seemed to zip by, it was beautiful outside, it was mild outside even though it was only a week before Christmas.

As I drove up the street towards our driveway, I saw the cars parked out front and then I remembered that my husband had a bunch of his friends over to play poker. My hopes of a nice quiet (or not so quiet) night in the bedroom with my husband pretty much subsided as I turned into the driveway. I got out of the car and walked in to my husband and his friends hollering at the football game on TV while enjoying their poker game; it was obvious that most of them were drunk already. I saw a case of beer on the table so I helped myself and opened one, not caring whose case it was... it's my house too and it was infested with men... dammit!

As I went to the dining room where they setup the poker table, I sat beside my man and watched him as he enjoyed his game, but everyone's eyes were all over me a little more than usual. I looked down and made sure that everything was in order, which it was; well except that I was wearing a rather short cut shirt. I smiled and asked, "What?" to his friend Mark and he offered back a slight smile and said, "Nothing," as he smiled. Eventually people's eyes settled down and they continued to play poker.

As the night progressed and we all got a little more drunk, the poker game ended and we headed to the living room to watch the next football game. I got up to grab another beer and blocked the view of the TV from Brian for a few moments and he said one of his smart assed comments like he usually does, "Get out of the way slut! Do something useful like suck on my cock!" I don't know if it was the booze, or if it was how horny I was, but I blurted out, "Gladly, anytime and you know it!" Suddenly he stood up and unzipped his pants and let them drop. I froze.

Everyone looked at him and then at me. I could see his bulge in his boxers as I stood there frozen... although a bit nervous I wasn't going to just tell him make a fool out of me by putting it away this time like I always had before when he teased me in front of his friends. I was horny and the sudden thought of sucking him off in front of an audience really turned me on. Besides, the liquid courage was really helping in the "courage department" for me.

I gulped, took a few steps towards him and then dropped to my knees. I pulled down his boxers in one quick motion, acting quickly before my nerves could stop me. His cock bobbed out and tapped me on the nose and I, just as quickly, shoved it into my mouth and started to suck on his cock. I was still nervous as hell, but I decided that I was going through with it.

I heard him let out a noise then a moan; he sounded both surprised and excited. His cock was growing inside my mouth and it was causing my pussy to start getting wet. I peeked at his friends and I noticed that their eyes were all on me and their bulges were starting to grow in their pants. Wow... oh. em. gee! I couldn't believe I was doing this!

After a couple of minutes of sucking Brian's cock to full mast, I noticed that Mark had unzipped his fly, pulled out his cock and was actually stroking it. The other guys didn't seem to care, they were too involved in watching me in action. One of the guys muted the game so that they could hear my wet slurping noises as I took care of my man.

Suddenly, things took a turn. My husband looked down at me and said "Slut, you are ours tonight and not just mine, you understand?" I just froze and looked up at him, I wanted to say yes but I was in shock, I mean... his friends?

Before I could even mutter anything, I felt my pants being unbuttoned from behind and turned my head quickly to see Mark standing there, without his pants on and his rock hard cock bobbing near my ass... it was my call, do I stop it or do I continue?

My mind was unsure but my pussy was throbbing with excitement and the liquid courage was really helping me to ignore my inhibitions. I lifted my knees off the floor and let him pull them off. I got on all fours and continued to suck on Brian as I felt Mark's hard, long cock slowly slide all the way into my dripping pussy in one plunge. Ugh… fuck… it felt so goddamn good! I still couldn't believe I was doing this.

I heard his moans of excitement and acceptance fill the room as he was balls-deep inside my hot wet dripping slit. "Wow," is all I could think, I was in front of Brian's friends and sucking him off and taking Mark's cock at the same time. All eyes were on me and, god fucking dammit, I was enjoying this. I could feel that my husband was about to blow his load in my face so I slowed down while sucking him. He pulled his cock out of my mouth and let a couple of thick, warm jets of his cum spurt out of his shaft and they splashed down on my face; I could feel them dangling from my chin to my tits, long thick gooey strands.

Ugh… I fucking love cum on my slut face, it's always been a weakness of mine.

I looked around at Brian's friends as Mark continued to thrust in and out, with my mouth now vacant. Without a cock to muffle my moans, they were loudly escaping my mouth with every thrust. I looked up and around the room, realizing that his friends were all without pants and stroking their cocks. Clearly they were enjoying the show that I was the center of attention in.

Mark's strong hands squeezed my tits as his cock swelled inside of me. Before I knew it, I felt his cock spurting his load deep inside of me. He had an enormous load, it seemed like it was never going to stop. He filled me up with jet after jet of his warm, hot, thick cum… wow! It felt so fucking good! As he pulled out, his cum-covered cock bobbed in the air while I felt his cum gush out of my pussy, dribble down my legs and onto the carpet.

At this point, there was a bit of a lull which started to make me feel a bit vulnerable. I was naked and unsure what was to come next and a bunch of guys were just staring at me. Thankfully, Brian took control and fixed the awkwardness quickly by moving around and started to lick my cum-covered clit. Wow, oh em gee! It wasn't going to take me long to cum with this happening. My pussy was aching with excitement as my hole dribbled cum down over my clit. He was licking some other man's seed out of me. I had always fantasized about this, but never thought it would come true. It really fucking turned me on... to a height I had never experienced!

My head rested down on the couch for a second as I was being eaten. As I lifted my head for a brief moment, I saw Jason standing there and offering me his cock. I grabbed his hand and pulled him towards me and I licked the underside of his shaft. As my tongue teasingly licked, it bobbed in my face. Jason took his cock and rubbed it in some of Brian's cum which was still dripping off of my chin and then he shoved it into my mouth.

Eagerly, I sucked Brian's cum off Jason's cock. It was so creamy and tasted so good. My pussy was aching badly, and my orgasm was building, my legs began to tremble, oh fucking gawd... I couldn't hold it anymore... I came so hard all over Brian's face!

My whole body quivered as I lost control, my muffled moans radiated through Jason's cock as he face-fucked me. My pussy juices sprayed violently out of me and all over Jason. Jet after jet of my hot juices splashed powerful off of him, back onto myself and onto the floor.

Jason's cock tasted good and I was really enjoying being a filthy cumslut that night. I felt Jason was getting close to cumming, I looked up at him and he whispered and smiled a simple, "Stop" to which I obliged.

He stood up, walked around me and slid his cock in slowly; all the way into my pussy to the back of my walls. He caused the remainder of Mark's cum that didn't drip down my clit and legs to ooze out around his cock. Holy fuck, was he ever big, and the fattest cock I had ever been stretched by!

My pussy was incredibly slick and juicy; perfect for him to fuck. I could feel his prince albert gliding along my inner walls and causing me to be extra sensitive. It felt sooo good and, frankly at this point, I was oblivious to other people being in the room, so much so that when I raised my head there was another cock in my face.

It was Brian's friend Steve and his cock was already rock hard and dripping long strands of clear precum.

He smiled shyly down at me and at this point I was over the shyness. I just grabbed his delicious looking cock and shoved it where it belonged at that moment; in my slutty cum-eating mouth. I bobbed up and down on his cock, hungrily devouring his meat, my saliva drooling out and soaking his balls as Jason pounded away at my pussy.

God… Jason's fat cock felt so good in my pussy too... all I could think at that moment was, “I'm such a whore!” but I loved it! I was so sensitive from my snatch being filled beforehand and now being filled all over again. Steve's prince albert piercing rubbed my walls, increasing my sensitivity with every thrust. My moans echoed in the room as I was being fucked like the little slut that I am. Brian slid a mirror on the floor under me so I could look down and see all of Mark's cum glistening and dripping from Jason's shaft. Holy fuck… what a dirty creamy mess and what a hot view!

Steve's cock tasted amazing in my slutty mouth. I could feel his precum oozing out all over my tongue. He moaned and his legs writhed on each side of me as I continued to eagerly suck on his cock; only taking occasional breaks to lick his balls.

Once again, my pussy was tightening on Jason's cock, and I felt a rush surge over me, one that's tough to explain. My pussy exploded in delight as I had a full body orgasm. My pussy gushed juices all over and down his legs, but I felt tingles and waves of pleasure all throughout my entire body. I watched myself cum in the mirror as my pussy spasmed all over him and made a huge sticky mess all over the mirror, I must have squirted a couple of liters of nectar!

Jason kept thrusting and moaned loudly as he felt my juices went all over him. I felt a tongue invade my asshole, but it felt ooh so good. I looked back, over my shoulder to discover it was Clayton… wow what a dirty boy, my first encounter from Clayton was his tongue deep in my ass!

Clayton continued to tongue my asshole while Jason exploded in my pussy; nearly pushing me over from his hard thrusts as he shot a tremendous load of hot thick cum inside me. Jet after jet of creamy cum, I could feel myself filling up. His moans were very loud and echoed throughout the room.

When he pulled out, my pussy didn't even have a chance to lose any of his load, Clayton was ready and dove his cock deep inside me…. God fucking damn; I really could get used to being a well-used slut!

My pussy, already soaked, was making remarkably loud, juicy noises. The only noise that rivalled it were our collective moans as Clayton fucked the pool of blended cum deep within me.

Jason sat back down with a smile on his face, and continued to stroke his still hard cock; as he used Mark and his own cum mixed with my juices as lube.

While Clayton pounded at me, I saw Brian getting involved in the fun once again. He removed the mirror as he tried not to spill the puddle that I made on it. He then wiggled under me as he laid on his back. Carefully, with the help of his guiding hand, he slid his cock in at the same time as Clayton's was inside of me. I was taking both of their cocks as they thrust in and out of me, their cocks glided against each others. The feeling was so intense, my pussy was so tight and it struggled to stretch to fit two cocks in and the same time.

It didn't take long; my pussy escalated from quivering to full-on convulsing, I felt my inner walls tighten, I was quickly losing control. Suddenly it overtook me, it gushed and gushed some more. My warm thick creamy pussy cum dribbled down their shafts. I was in heaven, exhausted at the same time, but I didn't want it to end!

Clayton pulled out and put his cum-covered cock in my face. It didn't take any coaxing; I got busy and sucked on his juicy fat cock, covered in gobs of delicious thick cum, and I slurped them off as I cleaned his shaft.

My face, my pussy and my legs were soaked, I was literally a cum-covered slut and I was really enjoying feeling Brian's cock pounding my cum-filled hole as I sucked on Clayton's cock.

Clayton was writhing beneath my cock-hungry mouth as I went to town on him. I wanted to drink his load so badly! I had enough cum in my pussy; it was time for a treat to swallow. It was hard to stay focused with how good Brian's cock felt in me but I did my best. Unfortunately as Clayton got close, he pulled out and didn't let me drink his load. Instead he went around and they carefully adjusted their positions so that he could push his cock inside my tight little asshole while Brian continued to fuck my pussy. As they started to simultaneously thrust in both of my holes, before I could moan, my mouth was blocked with another cock.

Wow, at this point I remembered hoping that it would never end. I was getting exhausted but I was still so fucking horny, it was Max's cock and I felt Brian and Clayton's cumloads building.

I was rocking on Brian and Clayton's cocks when I felt them nearing orgasm. It turned me on so much, once again, I came down their cocks, while I gagged on Max's cock. I came so hard, my holes squeezed so tight that it triggered theirs, I never had a 3-way simultaneous orgasm before but let me tell you, it was so fucking hot. My pussy gushed all over the place as their loads filled my pussy and asshole to the brim.

As they pulled out, I got up on the couch and sat on Max's cock. I turned around to face the other boys and let them watch me ride him. I could tell from his moans and the throb inside his shaft that he couldn't take much more of this. His cock was stretching my juicy pussy as all the boys cum oozed down his shaft as it glistened from the globs of their seed beneath the glimmer of the ceiling lights.

I bobbed and bounced up and down as gobs of gooey cum oozed down his shaft. Max's cock was swelling up, I could feel it inside of me. I reached down to his balls and caressed them; rubbing all the boys cum into his nuts. This sent him over the edge and he unloaded deep inside my tender, over-fucked pussy.

What a night, so many loads all inside me... I was exhausted, tender and raw, dehydrated; and officially a slut!

This is only an intro as to how I became a slut. Little did I know that this was about to lead to decades of naughty, creamy, dirty debauchery.

University Menage - Threes Allowed

“Guys, I’d like to make a toast…”

A clink sounded from the side of a wine glass, and the members at the table stopped their small chatter and averted their eyes to the front.

EcoFriends, an environmental coalition organization at a prestigious university, successfully met the threshold of raising $10,000 in the past semester. The leader of this organization was Joshua Henrichson, who was standing at the head of the table at the restaurant, a wine glass raised in his hand.

Rebecca Norman, the leader of the correspondence team of the organization, couldn’t keep her gaze off of him as he prepared for the toast.

Rebecca was 21 years old, and although she was petite and reserved, she served as a forefront for the fundraising campaign. She was short, hailing at a mere 5’0, and had long, red locks that hung in the small of her back. Her emerald eyes glittered with passion every time their organization started a new project, and was always volunteering for extra side projects. Rebecca majored in Communications, which came as a surprise to some due to her nature. Ever since she was a teenager, she wanted to be a journalist. So, naturally she handled a lot of the correspondence for the group, and ran the blog that had a lot of traffic.

Across the table was another member, who was looking at Rebecca with a longing gaze. He realized that he was staring for too long and looked down at his plate. He was Elijah Lopez, a friend of Rebecca's, and was a supporting member who went back and forth between teams in the group. His skin was caramel brown with honey colored eyes, with his most pronounced feature being his Roman nose. He joined the organization at the urging of Rebecca's request, as he couldn't say no to her.

"I just want to thank each and every one of you for all of your hard work and support," Joshua began, his light blue eyes flickering to each individual at the table, "Through various bake sales, barbecues, football games, and other crazy events, we managed to meet our goal for the semester. Abraham, Jessica, Muhammad, Omar, Luli…"

Joshua gestured to each member that sat around the table, each one smiling and nodding in acknowledgement. His eyes averted to Rebecca, and his gaze softened with a smile. "And Rebecca, who has been an insane help to the group. You guys know how much she has done for us. We wouldn't be here especially without Rebecca with her outreach to the community and making people aware."

Rebecca's smile grew, and she could feel her heart swell in her chest. She nodded her head and mouthed a 'thank you.'

Joshua grinned and turned to the whole table, raising his glass even further to the ceiling. "So, to all of you, you made this happen! Cheers!"

Everyone raised their glasses and cheered with him, and resumed their dinner and chatter. Rebecca kept busy with a couple of girls beside her, and Elijah forked at the potatoes on his plate. Joshua made sure to visit with everyone at the table, expressing his utmost gratitude to the group.

Joshua met Rebecca's glance a few times with a boyish grin, and she'd have to turn away, a small smile on her lips. Rebecca has been crushing on him ever since their first project together. Joshua was tall, his dark brown, curly hair always slicked stylishly in some way, and had a sharp jawline that paired with his other sharp features. Freckles adorned his nose, which Rebecca made sure to note once when he leaned over her shoulder. He was always focused and attentive to everyone's needs and ideas in the group; he made sure everyone was heard and took part somehow.

Rebecca loved that he was so passionate about helping the community, and it was one late night at the library that made her fall for him.

They were going over ideas together, and as Rebecca was doing research on her laptop, she spotted him falling asleep in the corner of her eye. He was leaning into the palm of his hand against his face, his lips slightly parted. She couldn't forget how peaceful he looked, compared to his stressed, attentive nature from earlier. The hard line between his shapely brows was relaxed, and his focused eyes were resting. The normally slicked tresses of hair were rustled and unkempt from the long day. As she was gazing at him, the sliding of his elbow erupted him out of his nap.

Rebecca had put a hand on his shoulder, concerned. "We can schedule another session and call it early tonight, if you'd like?"

Joshua shook his head and had a renewed sense of concentration on his face. "No, no. I'm sorry. With finals, this, and stuff going on at home… it's been a hectic month. And… I'm just tired," He turned to Rebecca with a quite exhausted smile, "I really do want to finish this."

They had finished their research within an hour or so, and he walked her to her car in the parking lot, and made sure she exited safely. As she was driving home, that's when she knew she was starting to have feelings for him.

Currently, though, Joshua was cackling at something Omar said at the other end of the table, and Rebecca was visiting with the other members.

Elijah excused himself from the table and waited outside of the restaurant, scrolling mindlessly through his feed on his phone.

Elijah met Rebecca in their freshman year, in a biology class. They were assigned as partners, and he was nearly dumbfounded at how pretty she was. They were in the same minor, so they took the same classes sometimes throughout the years. They grew close as friends, and started to hang out outside of school. Elijah started to see how cheerful and sweet of a person she was, which further cemented his feelings for her.

Which was why he had to excuse himself. He couldn't stand to see her gawk over Joshua any longer, and it would twist his heart. Joshua was so clueless and dumb in his eyes, to deny or not see how Rebecca was longing after him. If Elijah were him, he'd scoop her up in a heartbeat. But he wasn't Joshua, and he certainly didn't have the balls to fess up now.

He heard the restaurant door open to his right, and he saw Luli rush out with her cellphone to her ear. Her eyes were alert and full of urgency, and Elijah picked up that something was wrong.

Luli spotted Elijah and approached him, and told whoever she was speaking to on the phone to wait. She touched his arm.

"Elijah! An emergency came up, and I'm not going to be able to take you and Rebecca back home. I'm so, so sorry." And with that, Luli turned and hurried to the parking lot.

Elijah frowned and slid his phone in his pocket. "…damn."

*

"…and he told me, 'well, son, you're not too bad of a talker, huh?' Joshua mimicked, his hands jutting out in front of him expressively. Joshua was visibly buzzed, with a soft glaze over his normally alert, piercing eyes. He was leaning against the table and talking to Rebecca, who was laughing behind her hand. The other members were starting to file out after eating, and it was just them two eventually.

"I mean, that is pretty impressive. You talked down to a congressman." Rebecca giggled, her hand resting on the table, inches away from his. His long fingers were so close, yet so far. Joshua had never revealed such a side to her. She learned that with a little alcohol in him, he was quite a talker. She didn't mind, however; she enjoyed seeing him rave about different things.

In the corner of her eye, she saw her best friend, Elijah, enter the room. He had a frown on his face, and she just knew something was amiss. She faced him.

"Elijah, what is it?"

Elijah approached them both and regarded Joshua with a curt nod, then turned to Rebecca. "Luli had an emergency and had to leave," Elijah had his hands in his pockets and was rocking on his heels awkwardly, "...and well, we're kinda stranded here now."

Joshua's expression became alert suddenly, and he stood upright. "Did Luli say what happened?"

"No, just that she had to go. Luli carpooled us here, so now we have to take a bus or something."

Joshua unlocked his phone and his fingers tapped at the screen rapidly. After a few seconds he put his phone back in his pocket. "I texted and asked her to keep me updated. And as for you guys... I can take y'all home."

Rebecca stood now, and shook her head. "You've been drinking… if anything, we should drive you home."

"It was just a glass of wine."

Rebecca squeezed his arm gently with a knowing look. "Joshua."

Joshua stared at the floor thoughtfully, then clapped his hands together. "Okay, fine. How about we drive to your place, I'll sober up and then I can take Elijah home?"

Rebecca looked at Elijah for approval and confirmation of the idea. He scratched the back of his neck, and sighed. "Okay. I'll drive, then. I know how bad your eyesight is at night, Rebecca."

Joshua grinned and playfully smacked him on the shoulder. "Thanks, man. I appreciate it."

They all started to head out into the parking lot. Elijah and Joshua were in front of her, chatting about small things. Rebecca followed behind closely, and couldn't help but smile. It was a surreal feeling watching the two men she cared about deeply just talking to each other as friends. Well, maybe not friends, but close enough. Acquaintances, probably.

She knew Elijah was apprehensive about joining EcoFriends to begin with. He was a shy guy who didn't socialize much, and she knew he only did it for her. In one of their minor classes, she urged him to join for a campaign, and he begrudgingly agreed. He groaned about how cringy some of the people were, and Rebecca could somewhat agree to his testament; but even so, Elijah stayed and started to warm up to everyone eventually. Seeing his transition warmed her heart, and she was proud of who he has become. Even offering to drive for Joshua was impressive to her.

They approached Joshua's car, and Elijah slid into the driver's seat after Joshua tossed him the keys. Joshua slid into the backseat, and Rebecca debated whether to sit in the back with him or in the front with Elijah. After a millisecond of debate, she slid in the backseat with Joshua. Her knee was hovering beside his, and Rebecca took note of the heat that emanated from his body.

Elijah looked in the rearview mirror, and she thought she could see a flash of something in his eyes before averting them to the front. "You guys buckled?"

"Yessir." Joshua saluted.

"Yep!" Rebecca replied, her fingers fiddling with her skirt.

The drive to Rebecca's apartment was not terribly long; she lived about 30 minutes away from where the dinner took place. She did manage to brush her knee against his as he talked to Elijah and she. It sent a bolt of excitement through her, and she made sure that he didn't notice with her conversation.

Eventually, Elijah drove into the complex and parked near her door. Everyone shuffled out of the vehicle, and Joshua had sobered up some during the drive. They entered her apartment, and Joshua did a whistle as they walked in.

"You know how to spruce up a place." Joshua grinned at Rebecca, and he made himself at home at the loveseat in the living room.

Rebecca turned to Elijah, and placed a hand on his arm. "Could you fix up some coffee or tea for him? You know where everything is."

Elijah looked at her with an unreadable expression for a second before offering a soft smile. "Sure, Beck."

As Elijah left the living room and headed towards the kitchen, Rebecca sat beside Joshua, but not too close for comfort.

Joshua scanned the room, in awe of her décor. "I really like your place. It's homey."

"I try. I've been here for a couple of years, so I wanted to come here and feel like it's home."

Joshua turned to her; his eyes full with gratitude. "Thank you for taking care of me. I know you needed a ride, but still. Thanks."

Rebecca placed a hand on his knee. "Of course. That's what friends are for, right?"

Joshua glanced down at her hand and looked back up at her, and Rebecca smiled at him sweetly. It looked as if he wanted to say something, but never did.

They stared at each other for what seemed like eternity before Elijah entered the room with a cup of coffee in hand. Rebecca withdrew her hand in a flash, and Joshua coughed to himself. He grasped the cup from Elijah and nodded to him before sipping at it.

Elijah sat at the recliner opposite of the sofa, and leaned back into it. "Well, what should we do while we wait?"

Rebecca shrugged. "We could watch a movie?"

"Sounds fun." Joshua added, readjusting himself in his seat. He was a bit closer to Rebecca now, their knees grazing each other again.

Rebecca pulled up some random romantic comedy on the streaming app on her television, and leaned into the sofa. She could see Joshua in the corner of her eye sipping at his coffee, his eyes glued to the screen. At some point during the movie, Elijah stood and went to the bathroom, leaving them both alone. It had been thirty minutes at this point. Rebecca assumed he was having trouble or passed out in her bedroom.

After a bit of silence between each other, Rebecca laughed a little. “This movie is kind of bad.”

Joshua chuckled, his previous awkwardness seemingly dissipating. “The acting is poor, for sure.”

She paused the movie and faced him. “How are you feeling by the way?”

“I’m actually feeling decent now thanks to your horrendous, cheap coffee.” He gestured towards the cup with a cheeky smile.

She playfully shoved his arm. “I’m a college student; I can’t afford anything else.”

Her fingers linger in the folds of his arm sleeve, and they locked eyes again. Rebecca wasn’t sure what was coming over her tonight; she was making lot of physical contact and as she was looking at him, she couldn’t stop looking at his lips.

The atmosphere in the room shifted, and they both had a wanting gaze in their eyes. Joshua's hand reached up and stroked Rebecca's red bangs, and had angled himself closer to her face than before. His other hand gently placed down the coffee cup at the side table, and then rested on her leg. His touch was delicate, and she closed her eyes as she felt his fingers graze her cheeks, neck, and back up to her chin.

Her heart was slamming against her chest, her body on fire at this point. She was starting to feel a familiar, throbbing heat down below as she felt his caresses. A part of her couldn't believe that this was happening; she had been yearning for him for so long. Finally, she felt his lips meet hers, and she was amazed at how gentle and soft they were. The kiss was merely a peck, and he pulled away from her, visibly red in the face.

"I-I'm sorry. I shouldn't be taking advantage of you..." Joshua stammered, running his fingers through his hair nervously.

"No, no. I wanted it. I... want it." Rebecca replied, surprised at her own boldness.

Joshua looked at her, mixed emotions crossing his features. After a moment of deliberating, he leaned forward again and pressed his lips against hers. His hands rested on her thighs, and every place that he touched was left with fire. Her fingers tangled in his hair as they kissed, and she felt herself leaning backwards until she was laying down on the sofa, and he was on top of her.

He pulled back again, and looked into her eyes. Rebecca could smell his scent; it was a mixture of coffee and spicy, woodsy cologne. His face was so close to hers; he felt his breath on her skin and strands of his hair tickled her forehead. She wondered if he could hear her racing heartbeat.

“Are you sure about this?”

Rebecca nodded, and pulled his face towards her by cupping the back of his neck. They kissed again, and this time she felt his tongue enter her mouth. Her tongue flicked his own, and they did a slow dance as their bodies were pressed together. She felt his hand run up her thigh and undo the buttons of her skirt, pushing the fabric down around her knees. She kicked off the skirt and unbuttoned her blouse, exposing her modest breasts to him.

Joshua pulled away once again, and started to unbuckle his belt. He looked down at her as he removed his clothing, and exposed his athletic build to her. His broad shoulders dipped into his chiseled chest, and a six pack that was highlighted by the shadows of the room. Her eyes then trailed down to his briefs, where she could see his erection poking through them.

Rebecca felt dominated by his sheer size as he hovered over her, and pushed down his briefs. His dick was somewhat hard, and her hand reached out to stroke him. She was surprised at how hot and veiny he was, and she felt him get harder underneath her grasp.

Joshua was… large. He was a tall, athletic man, and his dick was not exempt from his size. It looked to be maybe eight or nine inches hard, and she was almost hesitant about it entering her.

They started to kiss again, and she felt his dick rub against her thigh. Reaching down with her fingers, Rebecca moved her white, lace panties to the side, and gestured for him to get closer. She felt his head settle at her entrance, at this point she was wet and hot for him. He gazed into her eyes as he slowly entered her, and Rebecca's mouth opened in surprise at his girth.

She felt herself stretch immensely around his size, and she arched her back at the sensation.

"Ah…" She moaned softly, and was cut off by his kiss. He thrusted himself into her depths, and she could see his eyes shut tightly from the sensation. Looking up at him was surreal; the man she loved was inside her, pleasing her, and she was pleasing him. They were one, and she reveled in it as her fingers caressed his chest.

Rebecca's eyes averted to the side, and her heart froze in her chest. She saw Elijah standing there in the hallway, his hand stroking his groin over his jeans. Joshua followed Rebecca's gaze, and stopped in his tracks.

"Elijah…" Rebecca simply said, not sure what to say.

"We thought you were asleep." Joshua withdrew himself and kneeled on the sofa awkwardly.

"Come here, Elijah." Rebecca gestured him over, and Elijah reluctantly obliged. She sat up, completely nude. She didn't feel uncomfortable being exposed to him for some reason, however.

He stood at the edge of the sofa. Rebecca stood and cupped his cheek. "Did you want to join?"

Joshua and Elijah shook their head in surprise, and both said: "What?"

Rebecca shrugged with a smile. "Why not? We all are friends and trust each other. We could have fun."

Joshua and Elijah exchanged looks, and Elijah's face was beet red. "I-I don't know."

Rebecca turned to Joshua. “Then, we will continue and you can decide whether to stay or not.”

Joshua seemed hesitant, but didn’t seem to be too withdrawn from the moment, so he obliged to Rebecca. They started to kiss once again and descended back into the sofa, with Elijah awkwardly standing there.

Elijah was still visibly hard through his pants, and he hesitated. Rebecca reached a hand out as they kissed and began to rub over Elijah’s erection, locking eye contact with him. She held the contact as Joshua entered her again, his girth still overwhelming to her. She winced at the size, but got accustomed to it as he started to pump into her a few times. Elijah seemed to have conceded to Rebecca’s idea and began to shove down his jeans.

Elijah’s dick revealed itself after he removed his boxers, and while it wasn’t as big as Joshua’s, it was still a good size at roughly six inches. He was fully erect, and twitched at the sight of Rebecca and Joshua fucking.

Joshua turned Rebecca over to where she was on all fours, in doggy style. Her arms were propped up against the arm of the sofa, and her head leaned forward over the edge. Each thrust made Rebecca let out a shaky moan, and she saw Elijah’s dick appear before her.

"Can you...?" Elijah asked in a soft voice, his face still red.

Rebecca grinned and gripped the base of his dick, which had an interesting curvature to it, she noticed. Her pouty lips planted at the head of his dick, and slowly descended to the base of him with her mouth. She felt his dick touch the entrance of her throat, and heard him moan at the sensation. She was being filled up with Joshua deep into her pussy, and Elijah's dick down her throat. She gagged as she sucked him off, spit accumulating in the corners of her mouth.

Elijah's hands ran through her hair and descended down towards her breasts, squeezing her nipple gently. Rebecca was moaning as Joshua was pounding into her now more forcefully, the tip of his dick hitting her cervix ever so slightly. Joshua was moaning a little, his big hands gripping her ass cheeks tightly.

It was a weird feeling, having two men she cared about fill her up completely on both ends of her body. Looking up at Elijah, her best friend, as he pumped himself down her throat, was erotic. The vulnerability in his eyes as he was completely exposed to her seemed to turn her on even more. And Joshua, who she had romantic feelings for, was close to cumming in the depths of her pussy by his erratic thrusts.

Joshua pulled out quickly, and spurts of his hot cum sprayed across her back. She felt the substance hit her ass cheeks as well, and dribbling down between her thighs. Elijah kept going, however, until his hips buckled and spurts of cum shot down her throat. He withdrew his dick and strings of cum and spit trailed behind on her parted lips. She swallowed the remainder of it like honey.

"You guys came and I didn't. My turn," Rebecca commanded, and splayed herself across the sofa, legs wide, "I want you to fuck me in both of my holes."

Elijah looked at Joshua in a questioning manner, as if to ask which hole is whose. Joshua finally picked Rebecca up and laid below her, his arms wrapped around her small waist. His dick was angled at her asshole, and slowly slid inside. Rebecca's head drew back in a moan as Joshua hands gripped her breasts, thrusting in her ass ever so slightly to get her accustomed to it.

Meanwhile Elijah settled himself in between her legs, and marveled at her body. This was what he always wanted, and her small, naked body was there for him to fuck endlessly. He adjusted his dick to where it sat over her clit, and ran the head of her clit curiously. Rebecca was bouncing to Joshua's thrusts, her small breasts jiggling with it.

Elijah slid inside her hot pussy, and moaned immediately at the feeling. She was hot, tight, and her pussy walls were already contracting from the fucking from before. Immediately, her pussy welcomed the new cock and tightened around him, causing Elijah to buckle slightly.

Rebecca was now filled completely in both holes, sandwiched between two hot bodies that were pleasing her, as she was being sent over the edge. Joshua's large hands squeezed and twisted her nipples, and Elijah's thumb was stimulating her little clit down below.

Elijah matched Joshua's pace, and Rebecca's eyes rolled to the back of her head. Her moans were louder now, she was almost screaming as they both pumped into her simultaneously. It didn't take long before her pussy walls contracted around Elijah, and she squirted her pussy juices all over his stomach. Her cum leaked around him as he pulled out, amazed at the thick, creamy substance that dribbled from her.

Her head leaned back against Joshua's shoulder as she recovered from the orgasm, her chest rose and fell with her deep breathing. After a few minutes, Rebecca ascended from the sofa and gestured for them both to approach her. Joshua and Elijah got up and stood in front of her, their dicks almost touching in proximity. They were both so close to orgasm, Rebecca wanted to finish them off.

She gripped both of their dicks and began to stroke them off, going back and forth between their dicks with her talented, slippery mouth. They both came at the same time, strings of their cum shot across her face. Jet after jet shot from opposing angles as they painted her beautiful face. Her forehead, cheeks and lips were covered, her nostrils were even full, thick gobs and strands landed in her long, beautiful hair. After their orgasms completed, they jerked out the remaining cum and then rubbed the heads of their dicks across her lips and cheeks.

They all were panting at this point, and Rebecca giggled. “Guess I have to clean up now.”

*

Joshua and Elijah ended up staying the night at Rebecca’s, both passed out in her bed, with Rebecca in the middle. They had exhausted themselves completely from the night, and Joshua nor Elijah had the energy to drive. Rebecca had cuddled their heads on her shoulders, and had a smile on her face as she drifted into sleep.

Things were definitely more complicated now, but that was a problem for later.

Follow *Emma Jade*...

Get notified when new books are released!
Visit bit.ly/emma-jade-newsletter

Check out other exciting stories written by *Emma Jade*... visit amazon.com/author/emmajade

- **Submission to My Billionaire Boss**
  After Nadia moves to a new city in an attempt to get away from an abusive ex, she finds herself a job as the executive assistant for billionaire Josh Sutton. With his help, she's able to finally get rid of her ex – but she soon learns Josh is after much more than that...

  Josh is looking for a special kind of relationship, one that leaves Nadia feeling unsure, but aroused. When she bites the bullet and agrees, it begins a long and exciting journey with a wide variety of steamy situations.

  From million-dollar yachts and mansions all the way to a trip to Paris, Nadia's wild adventures are just getting started...

- **The Vixen Voyeur: A MFF Menage Romance**
  What starts out as an innocent cycling ride, ends up in a voyeuristic adventure for Brian, a recently divorced gentleman who is struggling from an onset of loneliness.

  What becomes the object of his desire, quickly becomes a catalyst into a life he could never have imagined...

  Join us on this sizzling tale, where not one, but two sexy little vixens make Brian's dreams come true!

- **The Panty Snatcher: A Femdom Panty Fetish Romance**

  David has always had a panty fetish. His pent-up lust for panties controls his impulses. This time, it gets him in trouble...

  "He had just made up his mind to follow his instincts without shifting his yearning eyes from the fashionable unmentionables."

  Lisa, David's next door neighbor, catches him red-handed stealing a pair from her laundry. Not only is she going to teach him a lesson, she's going to have fun with it.

  "Firstly, from now on, you'll address me as Goddess. Secondly, I want you to strip for me."

  Delve in and enjoy this female domination tale and explore the world of panty sniffing, facesitting, underwear fetish, foot fetish and more.

- **Dirty Work: An Erotic Construction Site Romance**

  Sarah is a dedicated, hard-working foreman at a construction company. She is called upon when nobody else can solve issues at construction sites, traveling the country to fix messes that others have caused. Her dedication to her work and lack of time for any semblance of a relationship has caused her to be incredibly lonely.

  Grant is a construction worker, an uneducated street kid turned construction worker who never knew anything else. He is straightforward, honest and hard-working. His friendliness and charisma enable him to rally his team to success.

  Sarah and Grant could not have been more different, but difference has no voice when it comes to sex and love.

  Delve into this erotic tale of fantasy turned reality. Get ready, you're about to get your hands dirty...

- **Indecent Grades: An Erotic Student / Professor Taboo Romance**

  Erika is about to fail a class that she desperately needs to pass in order to obtain admission into college.

  Professor Charles Quinn, a strict no-nonsense professor, won't bend the rules for any student, no matter how smart, beautiful or kind they are... that is, unless...

  Erika is desperate and she'll do whatever it takes.

  Can Erika gain a passing grade? Will she get to go to college? Can she break the professor's strict, no second-chances policy? Nobody has ever been able to before, but she has no choice, she's got to try.

  Envelop yourself in this exciting taboo student/professor erotica tale to find out...

- **My Memoir Into Submission**

  Amelia meets her neighbor, Josh, a friendly good looking man who turns out to have some secrets. These secrets lead Amelia from a life of mundane routine to one of excitement and fun; while sexually empowering her through her discovery of what she really needs, and who she really is - a submissive.

- **The Secret Cuckold**

  Nathan becomes a cuckold, but his wife doesn't even know it. Having his wife cuckold him, gets him off in ways he couldn't even imagine.

About *Emma Jade...*

Emma started writing stories when she was seven years old. She wrote essays, articles, and over two million words of nonfiction before turning to fiction in 2013.

She watched erotic romance authors having way too much fun, and after writing her first erotic romance, she was hooked.

She writes erotic romances based on her real-life experience primarily featuring swinging, BDSM and cuckolding.

Emma lives near Toronto and likes reading, travel, and heavenly hash ice cream.

Made in the USA
Las Vegas, NV
26 March 2023

69697366R00059